This Little Tiger
book belongs to:

_____

_____

_____

To the little lords and ladies of Lumby –
Andrew, Daisy, Elizabeth, Grace,
Jack, Jennifer, Kate, Laura,
Samantha and Sophie
HR

For Venus, Matthew
and baby Esme x
MS

LITTLE TIGER PRESS
An imprint of Magi Publications
1 The Coda Centre, 189 Munster Road, London SW6 6AW
www.littletigerpress.com

First published in Great Britain 2002
This edition published 2003

A CIP catalogue record for this book is available
from the British Library

ISBN 1 85430 982 X

Printed in China

2 4 6 8 10 9 7 5 3 1

The Princess's Secret Letters

Hilary Robinson

illustrated by Mandy Stanley

LITTLE TIGER PRESS
LONDON

Last year I sent Princess Isabella a birthday card.

To Her Royal Highness
Princess Isabella

Happy Birthday
Love from Lucy +++
(38 Sunny Close, Townsville)

P.S. My birthday is on the
same day as yours.

P.P.S. What do princesses eat
at birthday parties?

Dear Lucy

Her Royal Highness Princess Isabella has asked me to write and thank you for your card. She is thrilled to learn that you share the same birthday.

Her Royal Highness has also asked me to say that, officially, the birthday menu includes cucumber sandwiches (no crusts), fruit cake and scones.

But secretly, the
Princess eats . . .

pizza!

38 Sunny
Close,
Townsville.

Dear Princess Isabella

Thank you for your letter.
I like pizzas too! Can you tell
me, do you have an entertainer
at your party? I have
TRICKY TREVOR - the magic
man at mine. He makes
gigantic monkeys
from balloons.
Love Lucy x x

Yum

PALACE

Dear Lucy

Her Royal Highness has asked me to write
and say that, officially, her birthday party is
celebrated in the Grand Ballroom.

But secretly, Princess Isabella and
her friends are entertained by . . .

DJ Dan the Disco Man!

38 Sunny
Close,
Townsville.

Dear Princess Isabella, x x x xx

Thank you for your letter. I can do the TWIST. I was wondering what presents princesses get for their birthdays. Do you get colouring books?

Love Lucy
x x x x x x

Her Roy
The Royal Palac
Princessville.

Dear Lucy

Her Royal Highness Princess Isabella has asked me to inform you that, officially, she receives silver candlesticks and teapots on her birthday.

But secretly, the King gives her . . .

rollerblades!

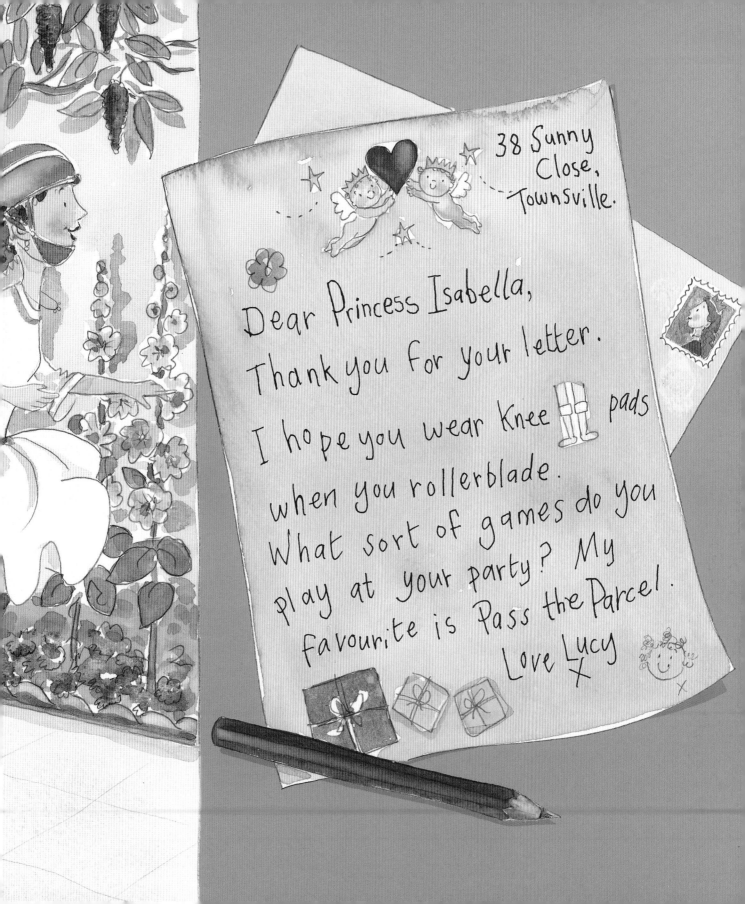

38 Sunny
Close,
Townsville.

Dear Princess Isabella,
Thank you for your letter.
I hope you wear knee pads
when you rollerblade.
What sort of games do you
play at your party? My
favourite is Pass the Parcel.
Love Lucy
X

Dear Lucy

Her Royal Highness has asked me to write to say that, officially, a princess is too busy to play party games. She waves to people from her carriage.

But secretly, the Princess Isabella likes to play . . .

musical chairs!

This year I sent Princess Isabella
an invitation to my party.

Lucy...

...would like to invite

Her Royal Highness

Princess Isabella

to her birthday party

on April 26th

3·00 – 5·00pm

special menu –PIZZA!–

yummy

I didn't think the Princess would be able to come to my party. Even so, she was kind enough to send me a parcel for my favourite game. Underneath the last wrapper was a little letter . . .

Dear Lucy

Her Royal Highness Princess Isabella has asked
me to inform you that she loves secrets . . .

especially secret visits!

Put some sparkle in your life with books from Little Tiger Press

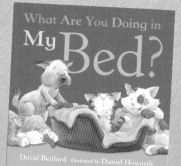

For information regarding any of the above titles
or for our catalogue, please contact us:
Little Tiger Press, 1 The Coda Centre, 189 Munster Road,
London SW6 6AW Tel: 020 7385 6333
Fax: 020 7385 7333 E-mail: info@littletiger.co.uk
www.littletigerpress.com